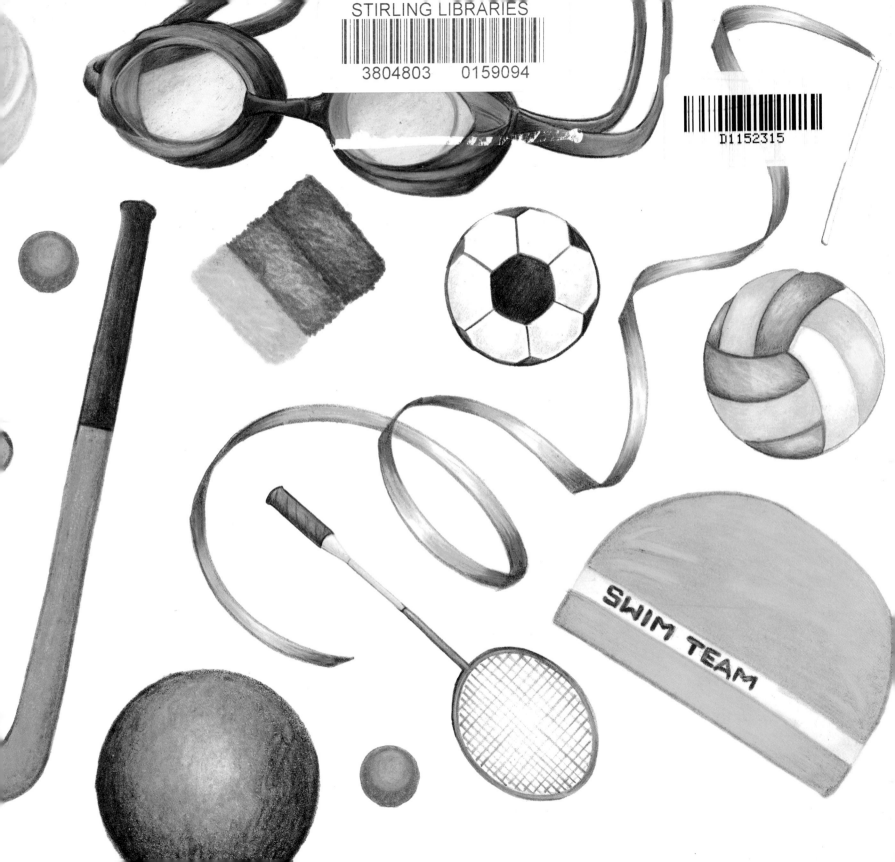

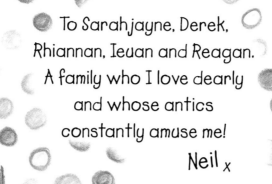

To Sarahjayne, Derek,
Rhiannan, Ieuan and Reagan.
A family who I love dearly
and whose antics
constantly amuse me!

Neil x

Red Robin
BOOKS
Where story matters

Red Robin Books is an imprint of Corner To Learn Limited

Published by
Corner To Learn Limited
Willow Cottage • 26 Purton Stoke • Swindon • Wiltshire SN5 4JF • UK

ISBN: 978-1-905434-96-1

First published in the UK 2012
Text © Neil Griffiths 2012
Illustrations © Janette Louden 2012

Design by
David Rose

Printed in China

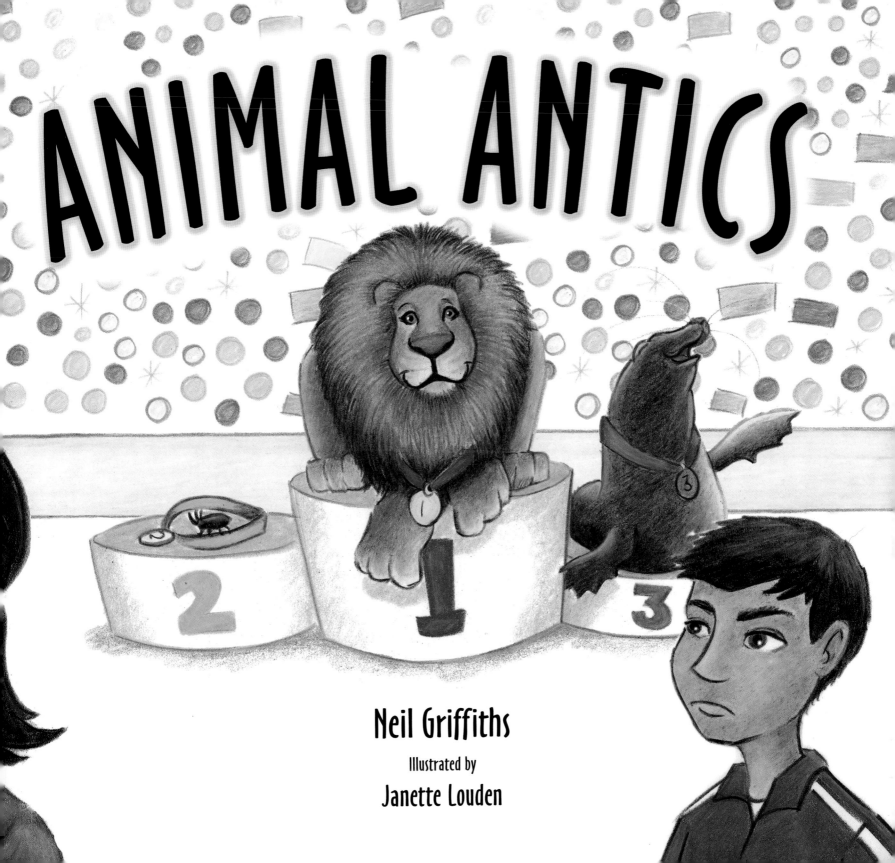

ANIMAL ANTICS

Neil Griffiths

Illustrated by

Janette Louden

A large crowd had gathered
outside the offices of the
World Sports Week committee,
eagerly awaiting an important decision.
The committee had been scrutinising and deliberating throughout
the night. They had rummaged out, sifted through, raked over, read,

Finally, the door of the office flew open and out stepped the rather ruffled and red-faced president of the committee.
"Despite our best efforts to decide otherwise, the committee reluctantly announce that the Animal Kingdom can indeed enter World Sports Week," he declared.

He was going to carry on, but was drowned out by the cheering, well, roaring, snorting, squawking, trumpeting and chirping of the animal crowd that had gathered. They leapt into the air and trotted, hopped, fluttered, stomped and paddled with excitement.

After months of training, the animals were fighting fit, finely tuned and ready for the competition. (Well, almost all of them were!)

But that's when the trouble began! Even the opening ceremony would prove to be difficult. First, there was confusion over which country each animal should parade with. It was easy with the red kangaroo, as it's only found in Australia, and the ring-tailed lemur, which lives only on the island of Madagascar.

However, arguments began over the African elephant, as it was discovered that these creatures could be found in 37 African countries. So it ended up parading alone, wearing all 37 flags!

Then a row erupted between the teams from the USA, Canada and Mexico over a skunk. Things nearly turned nasty when it threatened to cause a stink!

But that was only the beginning of the chaos.
None of the competitors would march with the crocodile or
the gorilla, as they were too scared. Then the dolphins didn't
know who to parade with. Despite their intelligence, they
were totally confused about where they actually lived
because they were constantly on the move, swimming
around the world's oceans!

The fleas and leafcutter ants were highly upset as two of them got stepped on, and none of the crowd could see them anyway!

After much to-ing and fro-ing, the parade finally ended with a baboon marching in with Zimbabwe. The competition could begin!

JUMBO SCREEN

Well, the organising committee may have breathed a sigh of relief, but their troubles were far from over. The early events were a clear indication of how the competitions were going to unfold. Things began disastrously at the Aquatic Centre. Almost every event was won by either a shark or a piranha, as no other competitors would enter the water.

There was a similar problem over at the Rowing and Canoe Lake, where other boats were too terrified to overtake a crocodile.

Some creatures dominated more than one event, as they seemed to have a huge advantage over the other competitors. An octopus was an example of this, winning the handball, table tennis and tennis events, not to mention the taekwondo, where it left everyone stunned. Literally!

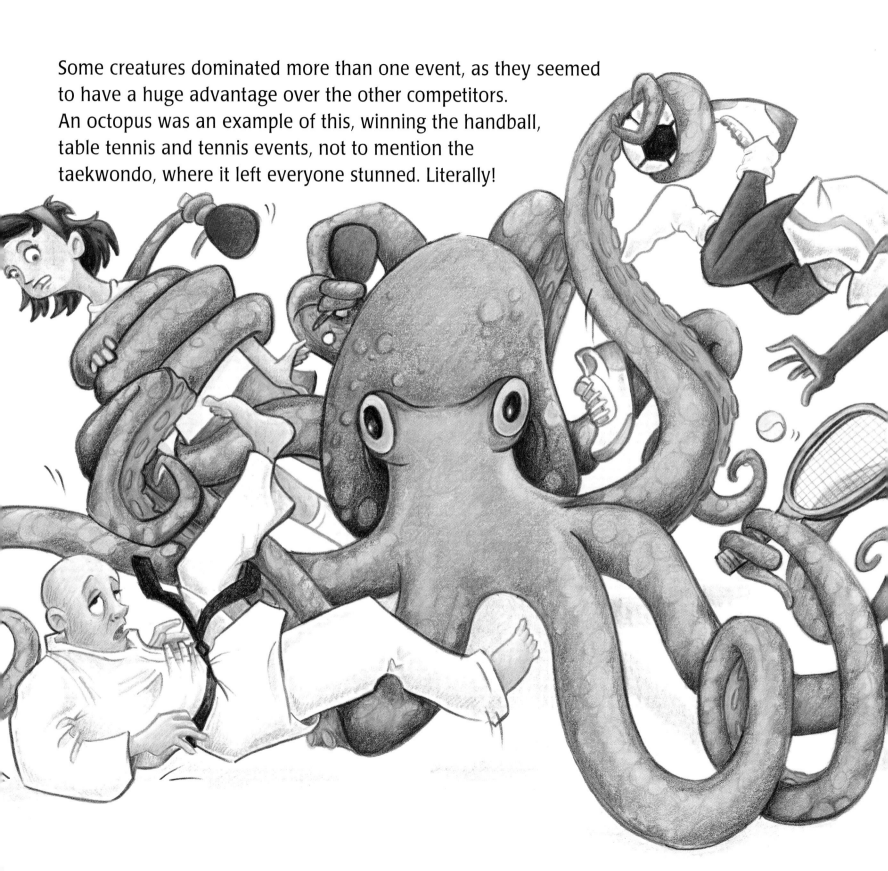

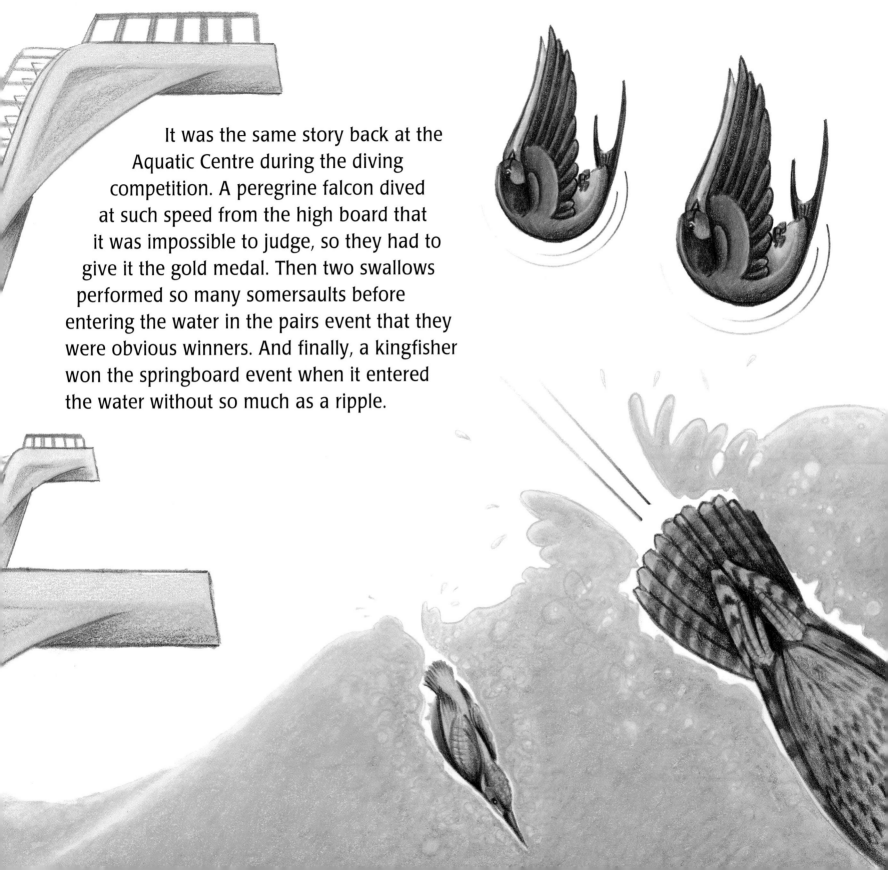

It was the same story back at the Aquatic Centre during the diving competition. A peregrine falcon dived at such speed from the high board that it was impossible to judge, so they had to give it the gold medal. Then two swallows performed so many somersaults before entering the water in the pairs event that they were obvious winners. And finally, a kingfisher won the springboard event when it entered the water without so much as a ripple.

Three events had to be abandoned completely due to the unruly behaviour of several animals. In the archery, a highly excited rhino couldn't hold back and hurtled forward, followed by an over-eager reindeer. As neither could be prised out of the targets, the tournament organisers had no option but to cancel the day's proceedings.

Similarly, all cycling races were postponed in the Velodrome, following the evacuation of the entire building due to a skunk!

But worst of all was the shooting competition. Two parrots and a mynah bird refused to stop talking and were such a distraction to the competitors that for safety reasons, the event was forced to a close.

Not all events, however, were such a disaster. The crowds were mesmerised by the tropical fish, anemones and swans that took gold, silver and bronze in the synchronised swimming.

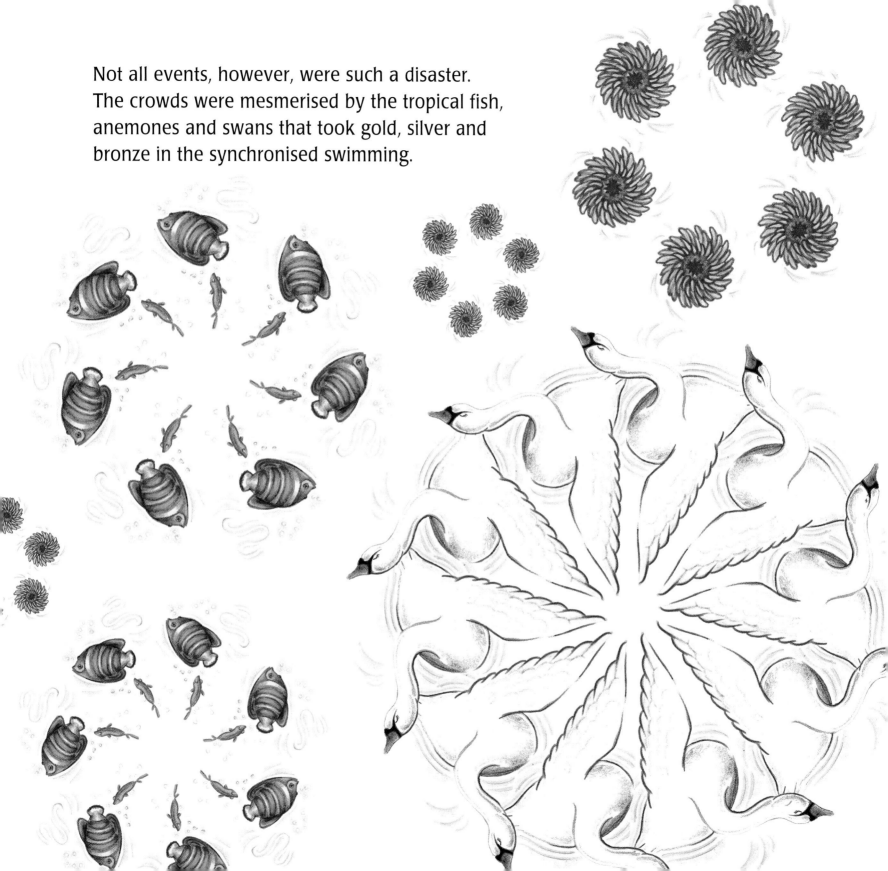

There was also a spectacular display by a peacock in the rhythmic gymnastics section, followed by fine performances from a bird of paradise and a flamingo.

As the days progressed, the organisers were bombarded with complaints. In the wrestling, everyone moaned that a gorilla and a bear were too aggressive. It was the same story at the boxing, where a kangaroo knocked out all of its opponents, and the referee twice!

There were injuries too at the Football and Hockey Stadium where several armadillos, a tortoise and two hedgehogs invaded the pitch, causing total confusion!

Then at the judo, it took several hours to release a competitor from a boa constrictor who refused to let go!

To make matters worse, several countries flew their teams home in a huff, as they felt humiliated by the dolphins who swam circles around them in the water polo, and by the seals who made fools of everyone in the basketball, volleyball and beach volleyball events.

Even the weightlifting ended in a protest, when the judges were forced to give the gold medal to the rhinoceros beetle who lifted 850 times its body weight, and the silver medal to a leafcutter ant who managed 50 times its weight.

There was pandemonium at the equestrian events when someone from the crowd stupidly shouted, "Look out, there's a lion about!", sending the zebra into a blind panic. It finished the cross-country course so quickly that the officials could barely time it. In fact, the zebra still hasn't received its gold medal as it has never been seen since.

Then as a protest and in support of the poor zebra, the horses went on strike during the show jumping and modern pentathlon competitions, making both impossible to complete!

Thankfully, all seemed to be going well at the badminton tournament until a flock of hummingbirds caused total confusion and left several players concussed.

Fortunately, very few moans and groans came from the Gymnastics Arena, as both the competitors and the crowd watching sat in total awe of the monkeys, lemurs, gibbons and baboons who swept the board, winning all the medals.

There was great admiration too for the ingenuity of a skate which, with the help of its offspring, dominated the sailing and windsurfing.

Similar astonishment was experienced at the trampoline contest, where a tiger proved it really could bounce, and a frog sprang so high that it had to be peeled off the ceiling!

It soon became clear that the animals were winning almost every event and it couldn't have been more obvious than in the athletics. A cheetah thrashed everyone in the sprints, and a giraffe won the pole vaulting and high jump with very little effort.

A kangaroo only took one hop in the hop, skip and jump event to take gold, and an elephant broke all records in the shot put.

Even when it looked like a human had beaten the anteater in the 400 metres, a photo showed it had actually won by a nose. It also looked as if a human was going to win the triathlon, as the gazelle had struggled with the swimming and cycling, but it then hurtled past everyone to the finishing line in the running section.

An ostrich 'walked' the walking event, but the final humiliation came in the marathon, as it was won by a camel, which unlike everyone else, didn't need to stop for water.

The committee knew something had to be done. But what? Regulations were regulations.

At the closing ceremony, the president stood up before the tense crowd.
"I have an important announcement to make," he bellowed.
"As you will have probably realised, the Animal Kingdom has
won every World Sports Week event." The animals went wild
at this announcement (some a little too wild), whilst
the human competitors stood in stony silence.

"We would like to congratulate them for their amazing skill, speed and huge talent." (This was followed by more wild behaviour.) "However, in order to give the humans a chance of getting a medal, we have decided to give the animals their very own Animal World Sports Week!"

At this point, everyone went wild, especially the humans, as they now stood a chance of winning.

Four years later, the first Animal World Sports Week officially opened and the animals competed against each other on a level playing field.

The committee were surprisingly delighted with their new event, but realised they still had some organisational issues to smooth out!